I Love My Mum

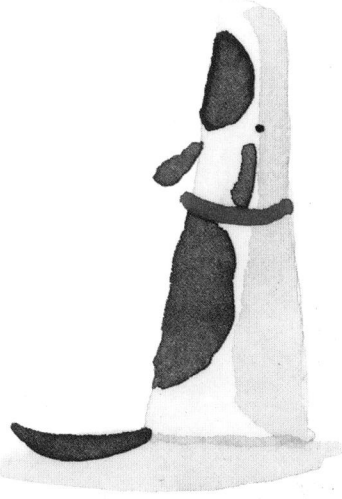

For Olive, Joseph and Sam, with love.

First published in hardback by
Scholastic Australia in 2009
First published in hardback in Great Britain
by HarperCollins Children's Books in 2010
First published in paperback in 2011

10 9 8 7 6 5 4 3 2 1

ISBN-13: 978-0-00-730916-0

HarperCollins Children's Books is a division of
HarperCollins Publishers Ltd.

Text and illustrations copyright © Anna Walker 2009

V1. I Love Ollie font copyright © Scholastic Australia Pty Limited, 2009
Created by One Eyed Dog Designs from hand lettering by Anna Walker.
Reproduced by permission of Scholastic Australia Pty Ltd.

Visit our website at www.harpercollins.co.uk

Printed in China

by Anna Walker

HarperCollins *Children's Books*

My name is Ollie.

I love my mum.

When I say, 'Mum, what will we do?'

Mum says, 'Let's try something new!'

We look

and talk,

we giggle

and walk.

We see a duck and a dragonfly.

We see orange fish swimming by.

We love to play

with the butterflies.

We love to hide in disguise.

At home we rest
our little feet
and Mum gives me
a special treat.

Mum says, 'Is that a fish I see?'

'No Mum, it's me, Ollie B.'

But what I love best
is my kiss goodnight.
I love my mum.
Sweet dreams, night night.